T0122220

PABLO AND LUCIA

MYRIAM M. MEDINA

To order additional copies of this book, please contact:
Palibrio
1663 Liberty Drive
Suite 200
Bloomington, IN 47403
Toll Free from the U.S.A 877.407.5847
Toll Free from Mexico 01.800.288.2243
Toll Free from Spain 900.866.949
From other International locations +1.812.671.9757
Fax: 01.812.355.1576
orders@palibrio.com

ISBN: 978-1-5065-4850-0 (sc)
ISBN: 978-1-5065-4851-7 (e)

Library of Congress Control Number: 2022916196

Print information available on the last page

Rev date: 09/29/2022

TABLE OF CONTENTS

INTRODUCTION:

Pablo and Lucia grew up in North Carolina. They had a happy childhood. They grew up in a home filled with love. Their nanny was a part of their life and they shared and enjoyed unforgettable moments with her.

DEDICATED TO:

The Hollands, and in particular, Jim and Andrea, for being exemplary parents and for all of the efforts that they made in educating their children as such loving parents.

1

THE SURPRISE

This is the story of two siblings, Pablo and Lucia. It all started when Pablo was four years old and super excited about his sister Lucia coming home. A new member of the family! His mom and dad had told Pablo how happy they were about Lucia's arrival... He was so happy!

2

THE BIG DAY ARRIVED

Lucia finally arrived. It was a huge event and everybody was very happy. Pablo was jumping with joy. Everybody huddled up together in joy to get a look at the beautiful Lucia, who could barely open her sky-blue eyes, filling her sweet face with kisses and affection. All the beautiful Lucia did was yawn...

3

THE NANNY

When Lucia was only a few months old, Martha, her nanny, arrived and took a look at her... and Lucia, surprisingly, smiled. "She's beautiful!" the nanny said. Lucia's hair had grown and she had golden curls and a smile that infected everybody. Her brother Pablo was responsible for making her laugh, with his jumping, antics and all sorts of somersaults, filling the house with laughter and happiness. Lucia would lift up her little hands as if she wanted to fly and her legs as if she wanted to jump over smiles and even more smiles. It made Pablo very happy when Lucia celebrated his actions. Plus, Pablo's imagination was limitless when it came to making his beloved sister laugh.

4

PABLO'S STORIES

Pablo was very creative. He had infinite Lego and wood blocks that his grandfather had made and brought for him during one of his visits. It was very entertaining to watch him play and he could spend hours playing. He made airplanes that landed on other planets or in other galaxies and while exploring other worlds, he saw how other children got on board for his new adventures. The nanny watched as Pablo played with his wood blocks with such focus... He was an expert at making pirate ships that conquered new worlds. Lucia followed him with her eyes, adopting a look of astonishment at every move Pablo made. She admired her brother...

5

PABLO AND LUCIA IN THE PARK

The mornings and afternoons were the perfect time for going to the park. Pablo went to school and while he was there, Lucia made the most of the time on the swings. She liked them a lot, with smiles and even more smiles. Lucia was a very happy girl. Her nanny would tell her, "Higher, even higher, until you reach the trees, higher, higher, higher! Until you get to where the birds are flying. If you don't stop, you can fly, beautiful Lucia." The wind would brush against her face and her golden curls would shine in the reflection of the sun... What a beautiful time! In the afternoon, when Pablo would finish school, they could play together. "Run Lucia, run; Pablo is a ferocious wolf..." And then the nanny would say, "Let's go home, it's time for dinner. Give me a hug, I'll see you tomorrow."

The next morning after breakfast was time to take Lucia for a walk. She was always pointing up at the sky, saying, "look, the moon, the moon..." She was a keen observer and really liked flowers. Her favorite pastime was being outside. She grew up surrounded by love.

6

FALL ARRIVED

The leaves of the trees had turned yellow and orange and Lucia loved to trample the dry leaves, crushing and crushing them but stepping slowly to find Pablo, who would hide his entire body under the leaves to surprise her without Lucia realizing. He would jump out from among the leaves and Lucia would open her big eyes with surprise and with a jump they would constantly throw leaves at one another. "I want to play as well," the nanny would say, and Pablo and Lucia would cover her in leaves saying, "You too!" But she would say "No, that's enough..." The afternoons were getting shorter and when the sun set it was time to go home.

7

WINTER ARRIVED

Lucia and Pablo were looking out the window, watching the snow fall, creating a white carpet inviting them to play! They looked at each other and smiled, accomplices on a new adventure! Wearing their snow suits they went out to explore together. Pablo threw the first snowball, inviting Lucia to play. Lucia followed his lead immediately until they were exhausted. After a while, they created something resembling a snowman with a carrot for a nose! Their dad took a picture to remember the day and their mom called them, telling them that dinner was ready and that they should come in because it was very cold out...

8

SPRING

It was a beautiful spring morning and the beautiful white and pink azaleas in the garden were just starting to bloom when the nanny and Lucia headed out to the library. Lucia liked to read and also liked to be read stories. Afterwards, they went back home to rest and take a nap. Lucia went to dance classes once per week. As enthusiastic as ever, Lucia would always say, "Let's go, let's go, I'm ready!" Pablo also went to taekwondo practice. It was entertaining to watch him. The nanny always laughed at his ideas: once, in a class, while the teacher was showing them the different positions, Pablo was distracted creating games in his head, and without him realizing, the instructor caught him. When he said "Pablo!" the boy jumped up and performed an oriental salute. Hahaha that was very funny.

9

THE LONG-AWAITED SUMMER

The years went by and Lucia and Pablo grew up happy. Lucia was fully aware that her birthday was in the summer, as opposed to Pablo's, which was in December. In North Carolina, it's very cold and can snow at that time of year. The family used to take advantage of the occasion to go skiing because they really liked the snow. July is the summer, the hottest month of the year. The nanny shouted out, "It's time to go to swimming classes!" Lucia jumped and said, "I'm ready!"

"You get prepared as well, Pablo," the nanny would also say. Pablo knew how to swim. He had to learn different swimming styles. That day's class was on how to float. Pablo got frustrated because he couldn't do it very well during the first classes. The nanny encouraged him, saying, "You'll be able to do it if you keep on trying, Pablo. You can do it," until he finally could.

July 25 arrived and Lucia was happy: her birthday had finally arrived. The house was decorated and there were games for the children. It was hot out and all of the children that were invited played with water. They had a lot of fun that afternoon. Lucia was happy to see her friends from school together.

10

THE GOODBYE

The years went by and Martha, the nanny, knew that the day to say goodbye was coming. She was going to miss them. She had seen them grow up and had shared many moments of happiness with them. Pablo and Lucia grew up filled with love.

Printed in the United States
by Baker & Taylor Publisher Services